La señora Asno se enfrenta a la Llorona y otros cuentos

Xavier Garza

PIÑATA BOOKS
ARTE PÚBLICO PRESS
HOUSTON, TEXAS

La publicación de *La señora Asno se enfrenta a la Llorona y otros cuentos* ha sido subvencionada por la Ciudad de Houston por medio del Houston Arts Alliance. Agradecemos su apoyo.

¡Piñata Books están llenos de sorpresas!

Piñata Books
An imprint of
Arte Público Press
University of Houston
4902 Gulf Fwy, Bldg 19, Rm 100
Houston, Texas 77204-2004

Ilustraciones de Xavier Garza
Diseño de la portada de Mora Des!gn

Garza, Xavier.
   [Short stories. Selections]
   The Donkey Lady fights La Llorona and other scary stories / by Xavier Garza ; Spanish translation by Maira E. Alvarez = La Señora Asno se enfrenta a La Llorona y otros cuentos / por Xavier Garza ; traducción al español de Maira E. Alvarez.
     p. cm.
   ISBN 978-1-55885-816-9 (alk. paper)
   1. Horror tales, American. 2. Short stories, American.
[1. Horror stories. 2. Short stories. 3. Hispanic Americans—Fiction. 4. Spanish language materials—Bilingual.] I. Alvarez, Maira E., translator. II. Title. III. Title: Señora Asno se enfrenta a La Llorona y otros cuentos.
   PZ73.G3678 2015
   [Fic]—dc23

                                    2015028680
                                            CIP

Impreso en los Estados Unidos de América
United Graphics, Inc., Mattoon, IL
septiembre 2015–octubre 2015
12 11 10 9 8 7 6 5 4 3 2 1

The Donkey Lady Fights La Llorona
and Other Stories

Also by Xavier Garza

Creepy Creatures and Other Cucuys

*Kid Cyclone Fights the Devil and Other Stories /
Kid Ciclón se enfrenta a El Diablo y otras historias*

Juan and the Chupacabras / Juan y el Chupacabras

Zulema and the Witch Owl / Zulema y la Bruja Lechuza

The Donkey Lady Fights La Llorona
and Other Stories

Xavier Garza

PIÑATA BOOKS

PIÑATA BOOKS
ARTE PÚBLICO PRESS
HOUSTON, TEXAS

This volume is made possible through grants from the City of Houston through the Houston Arts Alliance. We are grateful for their support.

Piñata Books are full of surprises!

Arte Público Press
University of Houston
4902 Gulf Fwy, Bldg 19, Rm 100
Houston, Texas 77204-2004

Art by Xavier Garza
Cover design by Giovanni Mora

Garza, Xavier.
   [Short stories. Selections]
     The Donkey Lady fights La Llorona and other scary stories / by Xavier Garza ; Spanish translation by Maira E. Alvarez = La Señora Asno se enfrenta a La Llorona y otros cuentos / por Xavier Garza ; traducción al español de Maira E. Alvarez.
     p. cm.
   ISBN 978-1-55885-816-9 (alk. paper)
   1. Horror tales, American. 2. Short stories, American. [1. Horror stories. 2. Short stories. 3. Hispanic Americans—Fiction. 4. Spanish language materials—Bilingual.] I. Alvarez, Maira E., translator. II. Title. III. Title: Señora Asno se enfrenta a La Llorona y otros cuentos.
   PZ73.G3678 2015
   [Fic]—dc23

2015028680
CIP

♾ The paper used in this publication meets the requirements of the American National Standard for Information Sciences—Permanence of Paper for Printed Library Materials, ANSI Z39.48-1984.

Printed in the United States of America
United Graphics, Inc., Mattoon, IL
September 2015–October 2015
10 9 8 7 6 5 4 3 2 1

This book is dedicated to my niece
Allison Rose Sanchez, welcome to the family

Table of Contents

The Donkey Lady Fights La Llorona

Clinging to his every word, we listen to Grandpa Ventura as he begins telling us a story.

"I first heard this story when I was but a boy," he says. "Abandoned by her husband for another woman, María went insane with jealousy. In a fit of rage she drowned her own children in the river to get back at him."

"No!" screams my cousin Maya. "How could she do something so evil?"

"After the madness had passed and she realized what she had done, María drowned herself in the very same river. For her horrible crime, she was cursed to walk the earth forever as the tormented spirit named . . . La Llorona!"

"La Llorona?" I ask. "That's Spanish for 'the Crying Woman,' right?"

"That's right, Margarito," he tells me. "La Llorona is a spirit with red eyes that burn like wildfire. Her hair looks like dancing snakes. They say La Llorona appears near rivers and creeks, looking for lost children to claim as her own."

"No way," says my cousin Luis.

"That's wild," adds my cousin Daniel.

"That's scary," chimes in Maya.

"What about you, Margarito?" asks Grandpa Ventura. "Do you think La Llorona is scary?"

Grandpa Ventura has noticed the incredulous look on my face. I love Grandpa Ventura's stories, I really do. But I am eleven years old now. I am way past believing in ghosts.

"Maybe just a little," I tell Grandpa, not wanting to hurt his feelings.

"Well . . . if you think that La Llorona is scary, would you believe that there are those who say there is one who is even scarier than she is?"

"Who could possibly be scarier than La Llorona?" asks Maya.

"Some say that the Donkey Lady is scarier," says Grandpa Ventura.

"Who's the Donkey Lady?" asks Daniel.

"The Donkey Lady is a *bruja* . . . a witch who lurks under bridges. They call her Donkey Lady because her head is that of a horrible donkey and her eyes glow yellow in the dark."

"What does she do?" asks Luis.

"She steals children as they walk across a bridge. She jumps out and grabs them!"

"No!" exclaims Maya.

"She drags them under the bridge, never to be seen again! But it's getting late," says Grandpa Ventura. "You all best be getting home before it gets too dark."

All four of us begin walking down the road that will take us to our homes. It's already getting dark, so we're all in hurry. Luis lives the closest to Grandpa's house, so he is the first one to get home.

"Don't let La Llorona get you!" he warns us before waving goodbye and heading inside.

"He's lucky to be home already," says Maya.

Daniel is the second of us to get home. "Look out for the Donkey Lady," he warns us before opening the door. He even makes hee-hawing sounds like a donkey before closing the door.

Now just Maya and I are left.

"Do you think that La Llorona is real?" she asks.

"Of course, she isn't real," I tell her. "It's just a story."

"But Grandpa said the story is real."

"Grandpa says *all* his stories are real," I tell her.

"You don't think his stories are all real?" asks Maya.

"I used to think they were, back when I was a little kid . . . but not anymore."

"Well, I do think Grandpa's stories are real."

"Well, they're not."

"They are too!"

"Besides," I tell her, "La Llorona isn't even scary."

"I think La Llorona is very scary," says Maya.

"The Donkey Lady is ten times scarier than the silly little Llorona," I tell her. "Only a baby would be scared of her."

"You think you're so grown up just because you're eleven," she says and starts walking faster.

When we get to Maya's house I can tell by the look on her face that she is really mad at me.

"I didn't mean it like that."

"Yes, you did!" she yells at me. "You think I'm a baby!"

"I'm sorry," I tell her. I genuinely am. I should have known better than to make fun of her. She doesn't like being teased.

"You're not sorry," she tells me. "But you will be."

There is something about the tone of her voice that scares me.

"I hope that both La Llorona and the Donkey Lady get you on the way home, so I never have to see your ugly face ever again!" She runs into her house crying.

Now it's just me left standing alone in the dark. I pull a flashlight out of my pocket. I point it in the direction of the narrow bridge I have to cross to get to my house. Underneath it runs a river, and it's not very deep. My cousin Luis and I come here hunting for turtles sometimes. It's then that I remember what Grandpa said about the Donkey Lady lurking under bridges. Surely he didn't mean this bridge. Besides, it's just a story, right? Slowly, I begin walking across the bridge. The wooden planks creak underneath my feet. Halfway across I notice that there is somebody else walking toward me from the other end of the bridge. As the figure draws closer, I can see that it is a woman dressed in white. There is something that doesn't seem right about the way she is walking. I aim my flashlight at her feet. It's then that I realize the reason the wooden boards aren't creaking underneath her feet is because she has none! She isn't walking across the bridge . . . she is floating across it! I point the flashlight up her face and see red eyes staring back at me!

"La Llorona!" I cry out. I turn around and begin running away from her and end up hiding in the water under the bridge. I can hear La Llorona calling out to me.

"Come to me," she tells me. "Come to me, child . . . come to me."

La Llorona is real, and she means to steal me away! I swim to the middle and submerge myself under the water, holding my breath so she can't see me. It's then that I notice a pair of yellow glowing lights swimming toward me. They draw closer and closer until I realize that those are not lights. They are eyes . . . eyes that belong to a woman with a hideous donkey head!

"The Donkey Lady!" I cry out as I burst out from under the water.

The Donkey Lady chases me out from under the bridge!

"There you are," says La Llorona as she catches sight of me. She grabs me by my shirt collar and starts pulling me up into the sky!

"No, he is mine!" hollers the Donkey Lady as she crawls out from under the bridge and sees that La Llorona now has a hold of me. The Donkey Lady leaps into the air and grabs my right foot and begins to pull me back down to the ground.

"I saw him first," says La Llorona as she tugs hard on my shirt collar.

"Finders, keepers . . . losers, weepers," snarls the Donkey Lady.

They pull and they tug at me as if I were a rope in a tug-of-war. They pull and they tug, they pull and they tug, until my shirt collar rips and the Donkey Lady pulls off my right shoe.

I fall and hit the ground hard.

Thump!

La Llorona and the Donkey Lady begin to circle each other. Are they really going to fight over who gets to claim me as their next victim? La Llorona makes the first move and pushes the Donkey Lady down to the ground. But the Donkey Lady is quick and jumps right back up. She then pushes La Llorona back.

La Llorona yells at the Donkey Lady, "*¡Aaayyy, mis hijos!*"

The Donkey Lady screams right back at La Llorona, "Hee-haw . . . hee-haw!"

The Donkey Lady then grabs La Llorona by her wild hair that dances like snakes and tries to pull her under the bridge! But La Llorona comes right back at her and grabs her by her long donkey ears. They pull and they tug, they pull and they tug. They go round and round until they go up and over the bridge and fall down to the water below!

Splash!

But even in the water they continue to fight! Seeing my chance to get away from both of them, I take off running as fast as my feet can carry me. I don't even bother to look back . . . not even once. I run across that bridge faster than a roadrunner ever could. I don't stop running until I reach the safety of my house . . . and lock the door.

Holes

"Your dog has dug holes in my yard again," says Mom. "You need to go clean up the mess he made, right now."

"Can it wait till after the football game is over?" I ask her.

"Now," she insists.

I turn to look at my dad, hoping that he'll run interception on my behalf.

"Don't look at me, Joe," he tells me. "Kenny's your dog."

"Kenny is *our* dog," I correct him. "We both went to the shelter to get a dog, remember?"

"I wanted to get a real dog," he tells me.

"Kenny's a real dog."

"He's a wiener dog," he reminds me. "People think twice about entering your yard when they see a real dog on the prowl. When they see Kenny, all they see is a walking hot dog."

"One of these days that dog of yours is finally going to go too far, Joe," warns my mother as she holds up the tattered remains of what had once been red roses. "When that day comes, he's going right back to the shelter!"

"Fine," I tell her. "I'll go and clean it up right now."

"You better find a way to control that dog," she warns me. "Why is he digging holes all over my yard, anyway?"

"Because digging holes is what dogs do," says Dad with a chuckle. "It's like in their DNA or something."

I walk over to the backyard and find Kenny digging yet another hole.

"Hey, cut that out!" I yell at him. "You're in enough trouble as it is already."

He looks up at me and whimpers.

I count seven holes in the backyard. "Why are you digging holes all over the place, Kenny?"

Kenny's ears suddenly perk up, and he starts sniffing around on the ground. He makes his way to a shed where my dad keeps the lawn mower.

"Stop that!" I yell at him when he suddenly starts digging again. "What is wrong with you, boy?"

Kenny whimpers a bit, but refuses to stop.

"I said stop it!"

I scoop him up and carry him over to the dog kennel we bought for him last week. I lock him up inside and start cleaning up the mess he's made of the yard.

"Kenny, what am I going to do with you? Why are you digging everywhere?"

"Maybe he's is looking for something," says Dad, standing at the door.

"But what?" I ask him. I look over at Kenny, who is staring at us pitifully from inside the dog kennel.

"Beats me," says Dad. "But just look at him, the way he's just sitting there looking out at the yard. He's definitely looking for something."

But what, I wonder? I haven't got the slightest idea.

"Whatever it is, you best figure it out soon, son," says Dad. "Your mom has just about had it with Kenny. If you don't control that dog soon, she just might make good on her threat to take him back to the shelter."

"Can I keep Kenny inside the house tonight?" I ask.

Dad scowls at the idea. "Can you make sure he stays off my couch?"

"No problem," I tell him.

"Then fine. But you best make sure I don't find one single strand of dog hair on my couch, okay?"

"You got it, Dad."

Later that night I grab some blankets and pillows from my room and set up camp in the living room.

"Time to sleep," I tell Kenny, who is sitting by the sliding door, staring out at the yard. "Don't even think about it, boy," I warn him.

He gives a low whimper before he walks over and lies down next to me on the floor. I doze off quickly, but the sound of Kenny scratching at the sliding door wakes me up. I turn to look at the digital clock display on the DVD player.

"It's five-thirty in the morning, Kenny," I tell him.

Groggily, I walk over to the sliding door, thinking that he probably needs to go pee or something. "Make it quick," I tell him as I start to unlock the sliding door.

"What in the world?"

Mom's yard is completely trashed! There are holes everywhere! What's going on? As soon as I open the sliding door, Kenny takes off and starts digging in the yard.

I'm about to yell at him to stop, when I hear Kenny snap his jaws onto something.

"Eeekkk!" A shriek comes from inside the hole.

I rush over and can't believe what I'm seeing. There, inside the hole, is what looks like a green finger!

"What did that dog do to my yard?" yells Mom. Both she and Dad are standing by the sliding door.

"I thought you said you were keeping him inside!" says Dad.

"There's something under our yard," I tell them. "Look at what Kenny pulled out from one of the holes." I hold the green finger up for them to see.

"What is that?" asks Mom.

"Ay!!" Another shriek!

Kenny begins pulling something green from one of the holes.

"What is that?" asks Mom.

Kenny begins barking at the green creature that is slowly rising up to its feet. Bald and green-skinned, with pointed ears, it stares back at us with red eyes. It hisses at Kenny and then gives out another loud shriek.

"Eeeekkk!"

Dad runs over to the garden shed and grabs a shovel. He swings it at the creature and sends it flying across the yard.

"It's either dead or out cold. It's an ugly little bugger. Look at that long pointed nose, and it's covered in warts," says Dad as he pokes it with the shovel.

"Is it a *duende*?" I ask Dad. Grandma used to tell me stories about green-skinned creatures with red eyes known for causing all kinds of mischief. She called them *duendes*.

"I don't know what it is," says Dad. "But it's this thing that has been messing up your garden," he tells Mom. "Kenny is innocent."

Hiss . . . hiss . . . hiss . . .

Suddenly there are hissing sounds all around us. We watch as one . . . two . . . three . . . four of those hideous creatures begin crawling out from the ground.

"Get behind me," says Dad.

Kenny starts growling at the creatures that have now begun to surround us. They bare their tiny but sharp-looking teeth at us. More creatures begin to emerge from underground. There are now five . . . six . . . seven . . . eight of those things surrounding us. They raise their claws up in the air as if ready to strike. That's when Kenny starts to howl.

"Arooo!"

"Arooo!"

"Arooo!"

It is a loud and piercing howl! What is Kenny doing? Suddenly the neighbor's pet terrier begins to bark. Our other neighbor's dog, a basset hound, begins to bark, too. Is Kenny calling for help? The green creatures now look scared. They make a hasty retreat and disappear back into the holes in the yard. Even the one Dad had smacked with the shovel is gone.

"Kenny saved us," I tell Mom. "He saved all of us."

The Gift That Is a Curse

"How in the world did I get so lucky?" I ask myself as I take one last look in the mirror. "I'm going to the eighth-grade dance with the prettiest girl in junior high. Just being seen in the same room with Terry is going to give me instant popularity points."

"I don't think you should go," says my sister Sabrina, who doesn't share the thrill of my newfound good fortune. "I have a bad feeling about this."

"You always have a bad feeling about everything," I tell her. It's true. If I were to listen to my sister, I would be even more of an outcast at school than she is.

"All that I am saying is that I have a bad feeling about this."

"Don't even start," I tell her.

"Start what?"

"This whole thing about you having a bad feeling. Just stop it already. How many times have we had to move in the last three years because of you and your so-called bad feelings?"

In the last three years we have gone to schools in Louisiana, California and Florida. "I'm tired of having to move just because something happens and Mom gets scared that people will find out what you can do. For once, I want to stay in one place long enough to make friends."

"But Trino," says Sabrina, "when have I ever been wrong?"

"I don't want to hear this." I know that her feelings tend to be right on target. But this one time I don't want them to be. "This is going to be my night," I tell her. "I won't let you ruin it for me."

"I don't want to ruin anything for you. But you know that I am clairvoyant."

There's that big, weird word that she likes to throw around so much. It means that she can see things before they happen. She calls them visions. I call them a pain in the butt.

"You know that I'm right, Trino."

"Why? Is it because you're like Mom? Because you're like Grandma used to be? Because you are a . . . "

" . . . a witch," she tells me, finishing the sentence for me. "Is that what you were going to say?"

"I was actually going to say *different*."

That, of course, is a lie. I was going to say a witch. My sister is a witch. There, I said it. She's a witch. A real one. It isn't something that she sought or wanted. You could say that it's more of a family tradition. All the women in my family have been witches. Some have been good witches who used their powers to help others. Some have not been so good and have used that power to inflict pain and suffering on others. Our grandmother was a good witch. My mother is one too. They all have the gift . . . or curse, depending on how you want to look at it.

"Why are you ruining this for me?" I ask Sabrina. "Why is it so hard for you to believe that Terry might actually be interested in me?"

"It's not Terry that I'm worried about," she tells me. "I like her . . . she has always been nice to me. It's Roy that I'm really worried about."

Roy is Terry's ex-boyfriend. He's a sophomore in high school and is nothing but bad news.

"They broke up," I tell Sabrina.

"Are you sure?"

"I'm sure. She broke up with him two months ago."

"But what if Roy finds out you're at the dance with her?"

"I'm not scared of Roy." Well . . . maybe I am, a little.

"He's nearly twice your size."

"Really?" I ask her, doing my best tough guy voice. "I hadn't even noticed."

"I don't want to see you get hurt."

"I know you're worried about me. But you really have to chill out, sister. I'm a big boy now. You don't have to protect me like when we were kids." My sister is two minutes older than me. That's it . . . just two minutes. Even so, she has always seen herself as my protector.

"Fine," she concedes. "You're right. I do worry too much."

"It's okay, sis. You wouldn't be you if you didn't. Will you be working the popcorn booth for the library?"

"Yes," she says.

I already knew she would. Sabrina practically lives in the library. She loves to read. Her dream is to one day become a writer . . . which I have to admit would be pretty cool.

"You're such a nerd," I kid her.

"Hey, it's not a crime to like books."

* * *

When we get to school, my sister and I make our way to the cafeteria that tonight will serve as a dance hall. When I see Terry and her friends, I tell my sister that I'll catch her later.

"Be careful," she warns me.

"You said you would let it go," I remind her.

"Hi, Trino," says Terry when she sees me walking towards her.

"You look beautiful, Terry," I tell her.

"You look pretty dashing yourself. These are my friends: Marissa, Sarah and Julie."

Julie just rolls her eyes at me. She's Roy's younger sister. "Charmed," she says, unable to hide her disdain for me.

"Nice to meet you all," I tell them.

"You're right, Terry," says Sarah. "He is kind of cute."

"Cute . . . like a puppy," says Julie sarcastically. The tone in her voice makes it abundantly clear that she doesn't mean it as a compliment.

"Your Sabrina's kid brother, right?" asks Julie. "They say that your sister's a witch."

"She's not a witch. Those are just stupid stories, okay?"

"That's not what I heard," says Julie, refusing to drop the subject. "I heard that she can cast spells and stuff."

Here we go. There's no escaping my sister Sabrina's reputation for being weird.

"She doesn't cast spells," I tell her. "She's just a normal girl."

"I wouldn't exactly call your sister normal," says Julie, smiling.

"What's that supposed to mean?" asks Terry. "Sabrina has always been nice to me."

"C'mon, Terry," says Julie, "admit it. She is weird."

"She is not weird," I tell her coldly. Sabrina and I may argue, but I am not about to let Julie make fun of her. She is, after all, my sister.

"I'm not saying it to be mean or anything," says Julie. "It's just that . . . why does she always dress so weird?"

"Weird? My sister doesn't dress weird."

"She's always wearing black, like somebody died," says Julie. "Plus she has no friends. All she ever does is read."

"It's not a crime to read," I snap back. Given the fact that Julie is failing reading class, it sure wouldn't hurt her to pick up a book once in a while.

Sensing the tension in the air, Terry grabs me by the arm. "Let's go get some fresh air, Trino."

"Your friend Julie isn't very nice," I say as we leave the other two behind.

"She isn't always like that. Julie is just acting that way because I broke up with her brother."

"I heard he still comes looking for you after school."

"He does," she tells me. "But I don't talk to him. Truth is, he scares me now."

"Scares you?"

"Roy can be super jealous. It's like he thinks he owns me or something. I had wanted to break up with him for a very long time, but I was just too scared to do it."

"Tired from dancing already?" we suddenly hear a voice ask. It's Sabrina.

"I didn't mean to eavesdrop on your conversation," she says. "I just stepped out to take a break."

"Serving popcorn getting to rough for you, sis?" I ask Sabrina. I know she is checking up on me.

"Hi, Sabrina," says Terry.

"Hi, Terry," she answers while placing her hand on my left shoulder. "I hope my brother here is being nice to you."

"He's being a perfect gentleman," says Terry.

"Trino, a gentleman?" questions Sabrina. "Trust me, Terry, you just don't know him like I do."

"Don't you have some popcorn to go serve?" I tell her.

"Fine," says Sabrina, "I'll go ahead and leave you two alone."

"Nice seeing you," says Terry. "We should hang out some time."

"Sounds like fun," my sister Sabrina calls back as she goes back into the cafeteria.

"You're sister is so nice, Trino," Terry says and leans over and hugs me.

"Get away from my girl!" I hear a voice scream at me. I turn around just in time to see a fist coming right at my face.

Pow!

The unexpected blow knocks me down to the ground.

"Get off him!" I hear Terry scream at Roy.

He punches me again squarely in the face. I try blocking his punch, but I'm too groggy from the first punch to put up much of a fight. Terry grabs Roy by the hair and tries to pull him off me, but he just shoves her away. I manage to stand back up, but Roy kicks me hard in the gut.

"Get off my brother!" I hear Sabrina scream as she jumps at Roy's back and reaches around to squeeze his stomach with both her hands. Whatever it is that she is doing to Roy makes him pull away from her in pain. He turns and runs away.

"Are you okay?" I ask Terry.

"I'm fine," says Terry. "Is your sister okay?"

My sister is sitting on the ground catching her breath.

"Did he hurt you?" I ask Sabrina.

"I want to go home," she tells me.

Once we're home, I ask my sister what she did to Roy.

* * *

"I don't know. I just remember seeing that he was hurting you. He got me so mad, Trino . . . I just wanted to hurt him so bad! All I remember is grabbing his stomach and then my mind just went blank. I don't even know what I did to him. I lost control, Trino, I lost control!"

It's never a good thing when my sister loses control of her powers.

The next day at school everybody is talking about the big fight I had with Roy. Not that it was much of a fight. I was the one getting pounded. But to hear people talk, I cleaned Roy's clock! I'm about to open my locker when Terry shows up.

"What did your sister do to Roy?"

"What do you mean?" I ask.

"You haven't heard?"

"Heard what?"

"It's Roy . . . "

"What about Roy?"

"Julie said that they had to take him to the doctor last night."

"What happened?"

"He kept saying that his stomach hurt."

"So?"

"Roy is dead!"

"Dead?!! What do you mean he's dead?"

"When they got him to the hospital, the doctors didn't know what was wrong with him. So they took X-rays of his stomach. The doctors couldn't believe what they found . . . "

"What?"

"They found snakes!"

"Snakes?" I repeat in disbelief. "He had snakes in his stomach?"

"Yes," says Terry. "He had snakes in his stomach. His intestines had turned into snakes!"

"But how can that be?" I ask her as I try to touch her arm. But Terry pushes me away.

"You lied to me," she tells me. "Julie was right about your sister. She's a witch. She did this to Roy!"

Terry is terrified of me. I can see it in her eyes.

"She's a witch . . . she's a witch," Terry says again and again as if she's losing her mind!

Even as I watch her run away from me I already know that come tomorrow morning, my sister and I will both be headed to another school in another city.

The Egg

"You say you found it in the cave behind our house?" I ask Dillon.

"Covered in leaves and branches," he adds. "It's as if someone had been trying to hide it, Mateo."

"What do you think it is?" I ask Dillon. "It looks like some kind of . . . "

"Like some kind of egg," he tells me, cutting me off before I get a chance to finish my sentence.

"Yes," I say, "it does look just like an egg. But it's so big." The egg is the size of a basketball. "What kind of a bird would lay an egg that big?"

"An ostrich, maybe . . . "

"What would an ostrich be doing in the cave behind our house?" I ask.

"I may not know what kind of egg it is," says Dillon, "but I know that it can do stuff."

"What kind of stuff?"

"Weird stuff."

"Like what?"

"Just watch." Dillon reaches slowly for the egg with his fingers, and little sparks of electricity erupt in the space between his fingertips and the egg.

"How did you get it to do that?"

"I didn't," he tells me. "The egg did it on its own."

"What kind of an egg can do that?"

"Maybe . . . and this is just an idea . . . I'm not saying that it is one . . . but maybe this egg belongs to a thunderbird."

"A thunderbird?" I repeat. "But those are just tales."

"Are you so sure?" asks Dillon. "Dad used to tell us stories of how people reported seeing thunderbirds all the time. Dad said that whenever clouds got dark and thunderstorms came out of nowhere, it was a sign that a thunderbird was near."

"There's no scientific proof that thunderbirds are real," I scoff.

"Then how do you explain this egg and what it can do?"

"I can't explain it, but there has to be a rational explanation."

"I'm taking it home," says Dillon.

"You can't take it home."

"It's my egg. I found it."

"But you can't take it home."

"Why not?" asks Dillon.

"Because Mom won't let you keep it."

"Mom won't even know that it's there," he tells me.

"She cleans our room every day," I remind him. "She'll find it."

"She won't if I keep it in the tree house outside. Mom never goes up there."

"I guess that idea can work," I say.

Mom is too scared of heights to ever climb up the ladder to the tree house.

"So how do we carry it home?"

"Like this," he tells me as he empties out his backpack. "Now place my books in your backpack, and I'll use mine to carry the egg."

Once home, we climb up with it to the tree house.

"Do you really think it's a thunderbird?" I ask Dillon.

"You're the smart one, Mateo. You tell me what else could it be?"

Dillon had me there.

Rumble . . .

"Is that thunder?" asks Dillon.

We both look out the window from our tree house and see flashes of lightning begin to dance across the sky.

"Looks like it is," I say.

"You boys need to come down and get inside the house!" our mother says calling up to us from below.

"Coming, Mom!" I call down.

Rumble . . . *rumble* . . . *screech* . . .

"What was that?" asks Dillon.

"Thunder," I answer.

"Thunder doesn't go, 'Screech.'"

Dillon has a point. Those shrieking sounds were unlike anything I had ever heard before.

Screech! There it is again.

"Look up at the sky," says Dillon. "What is that?"

In the midst of the lightning and dark clouds there is a figure flying that's the size of a small pickup truck. The giant pterodactyl-like figure becomes visible every time electricity is discharged from its grey wings!

"That's a dinosaur!" exclaims Dillon. "Is . . . is that what you think is in this egg?"

"I . . . I . . . I don't know . . . "

"Come down right now!" we hear our mother calling up to us again.

"It's going to get Mom," says Dillon. "She hasn't even noticed the thunderbird flying in the sky."

"It wants the egg in your backpack," I blurt out.

Dillon reaches into his backpack and pulls the egg out. That's when the egg begins to crack in his hands.

"It's hatching," Dillon says as he puts it down on the floor. We watch as a grey-skinned bird-like creature emerges from the egg. It waddles around for a moment, but then opens its wings far and wide. It rears its head up and gives off a high-pitched shriek. The newly hatched thunderbird begins to flap its wings awkwardly, but with each flap it seems to grow stronger and stronger, until sparks of electricity erupt and it takes flight. We watch as it flies up into the sky to join its mother. Then from the tree house we see the two creatures fly away.

"I told you boys to get down right now!" says our mother, who doesn't have a clue as to what has just transpired.

"Coming, Mom!" we answer in unison as we begin to make our way down from the tree house.

As far as our mother is concerned, this has been nothing more than a passing storm that disappeared as suddenly as it appeared. But Dillon and I both know better.

Grandpa Tito's Book

"The book is mine, Guadalupe," declares the blond-haired woman with eyes that seem as colorless as the moon.

"You can't have it," my mother, Guadalupe, tells her.

"You know I am the oldest, Guadalupe. The book belongs to me!"

"That doesn't mean anything!" argues my mother.

"What's going on, Mom?" I ask as I make my way down the stairs. Who is this woman . . . and why is she upsetting my mother?

"Nothing," says my mom. "Go back upstairs and go to bed."

"Where are your manners, Guadalupe?" questions the blond-haired woman. "Are you not going to introduce me to your lovely young daughter . . . and handsome young son, too?" she adds, turning her eyes toward my little brother Milagro, who is standing at the top of the staircase. He opens his mouth to speak, but no words come out. Milagro was born mute.

"Who is this woman?"

"Who am I?" asks the strange woman. "You mean to tell me your mother has never told you about me?"

The pencil-thin smile that forms on the woman's pale lips scares me. She steps toward me and reaches her hand out to touch me, but my little brother Milagro quickly runs down the stairs and pushes her away.

"No, Milagro," I tell him.

"Look at you," says the woman, staring at Milagro. "Barely a child, and already you are as brave as your Grandpa Tito used to be."

Grandpa Tito? Did she just mention Grandpa Tito? Milagro's eyes glare at the woman menacingly.

"Those eyes," says the strange woman, "I remember those disapproving eyes so well. You have your grandfather's eyes."

"It's time for you to go," my mother tells the woman sternly.

"Leave? But I barely got here, and I am not leaving without my book."

Our mother reaches for a salt shaker on the kitchen table and walks with it toward the unwanted visitor. For some reason the sight of the salt shaker in our mother's hand seems to startle the woman.

"You should have done this the easy way, Guadalupe," she warns our mother as she begins to make her way toward the door. "I want that book. I will have that book!" And with those words she is gone out the door.

"Who was that woman, and what does her being here have to do with Grandpa Tito? What's going on, Mother?"

"Get Milagro to bed," she tells me. "We'll talk then."

After I get Milagro tucked in, I make my way back down the stairs and find Mom sitting at the kitchen table. She's reading from a leather-bound black book.

"Is that one of Grandpa Tito's books?" I ask her.

"It is."

"Is that what the weird lady wants?"

"No . . . not this book. What Anastasia wants is your grandfather's special book."

"Is that her name, Anastasia?"

"Yes, Anastasia is my sister."

"You never told me you had a sister."

"Growing up, we were as close as two sisters could ever be . . . but everything changed after she tried to steal your Grandpa Tito's book."

"Why did she do that?"

"Because she was impatient," she explains. "She was the oldest, and the book would have been hers eventually. But your Grandpa Tito didn't think she was ready."

"When you say that the book is special, what exactly do you mean by that?"

"Whatever you write in the book becomes real."

"Whatever you write in the book becomes real?"

Those words reminded me of a time I was sitting on Grandpa Tito's lap at the kitchen table as he was writing in an old book. I remember him telling me that he had something to show me. He opened my left hand and placed a big, fat, hairy caterpillar in it.

Yuck . . . I remember how much it had grossed me out at the time. He then made me close my hand so tight around it that I could feel the worm squirming. What happened next shocked me. He told me to open my hand, and to my surprise the caterpillar had turned into a chrysalis . . . a cocoon.

"How did you do that?" I asked him. He didn't answer, but only smiled and told me to close my hand again.

"Open it now," he ordered.

When I did, a beautiful butterfly flew out.

"How did you do that?" I asked him in total amazement.

"Because I wrote it in my special book," he confided. "Whatever I write in this book becomes real."

"You said that Anastasia tried to steal Grandpa Tito's book?" I ask mom. "But she obviously failed to get it."

"Well, Anastasia did get her hands on it for a while and gave herself the ability to do magic."

"What did Grandpa Tito do when he found out what she had done?"

"He confronted her and took the book back, but when he tried to strip Anastasia of her powers, she turned herself into a giant owl and flew away."

"Why didn't Grandpa just change the story and take her powers away?"

"Because you are not allowed to change what somebody else has written in the book. Before he died, Grandpa

buried the book and told nobody where he had hidden it. He knew Anastasia would be too scared of him to come back for the book while he was still alive."

"But now that he's dead," screams Anastasia from outside the house, "I have nothing to fear!"

"She's come back," says Mom. "Go upstairs and stay with Milagro. I want you both to hide."

"You can't go out there and face her alone, Mom . . . she'll kill you."

"Do as I tell you!" she yells at me.

I run up the stairs to check on Milagro, but his bed is empty.

"Milagro!" I cry out. "Where are you, Milagro?"

"You don't know how powerful I have become," I hear Anastasia warn my mother.

I rush over to the window.

"I am more powerful today than anybody could have ever imagined."

I watch in horror as Anastasia's body begins to change right before my eyes. Her hands turn into talons, and wings begins to emerge from her back.

"My God!" I cry out. She's transforming herself into a giant owl!

"The book is mine!" she hisses at my mother. "Give it to me!"

That's when I see Milagro running in the distance. Where is he going? Anastasia lunges at my mother, and Mom throws a fist full of salt up into the air. Some of the salt falls on Anastasia's back, and it makes her hiss out in pain. The monster then reaches for my mother with its talons, but Mom manages to move out of its way just in the nick of time!

I grab my brother's baseball bat and rush down the stairs to help her.

"Stay away from my mother!" I scream. As Anastasia turns to look at me, I swing at her with my little brother's baseball bat.

Crack! The impact of the blow sends her falling to the ground.

"You can't have the book!" my mother screams back at Anastasia.

Just then a rock hits the back of Anastasia's head. It's Milagro! He's holding a shovel in one hand and a burlap sack in the other. He reaches into it and pulls out . . . Grandpa Tito's book!

"The book!" shrieks Anastasia. "Give it to me!"

Anastasia begins to flap her wings and flies toward Milagro. I scream for him to run, but Milagro just stands there holding the book in his hands.

"Give me the book," demands Anastasia as she gets closer and closer to Milagro.

Why won't he run? It's then that Milagro produces a red crayon from his back pocket and opens the book. He begins writing in it.

"ANASTASIA!" a voice suddenly screams.

"ANASTASIA!" the voice screams again. There is something very familiar about that voice.

"It's coming from the woods," I tell Mom.

"ANASTASIA!" the voice screams a third time.

"It can't be!" shrieks Anastasia. "It can't be!"

From the woods emerges the walking corpse of Grandpa Tito!

"ANASTASIA!" he cries out again. His voice is like thunder. "COME TO ME, ANASTASIA!" he cries out. "COME TO ME!"

Anastasia is terrified! She tries to escape by taking flight, but Grandpa Tito raises his decaying right hand up into the air and cries out, "STAY!"

Anastasia then falls down to the ground, seemingly frozen in place.

"Let me go!" screams Anastasia, but Grandpa Tito grabs her and drags her shrieking and screaming back into the woods.

They both disappear from sight.

"Are they gone?" I ask Mom.

"I think so," she answers.

"Grandpa Tito saved us."

"It wasn't Grandpa Tito who saved us," says Mom. "It was Milagro." She points to my brother Milagro, who has finished writing in Grandpa Tito's book and is now closing it. "Milagro used the book to bring back the one person whom Anastasia was afraid of."

"But how did you know where Grandpa Tito's book was hidden?" I ask him.

Milagro answers me by signing with his hands.

"Before Grandpa Tito died, he told me where he had buried the book. He said that if anybody could keep a secret it was me."

Milagro opens up Grandpa Tito's book and points to the first page. We instantly recognize the handwriting as belonging to Grandpa Tito. Written on the first page of Grandpa Tito's book is the following message:

"This book belongs to Milagro."

The Blood-Sucking Beast

"C'mon, you darn dog . . . go to sleep," I whisper to myself as I sit perched in a tree in the woods.

The night is getting cold, and I didn't bring my coat, but I am not going home without first sneaking up to my girl-friend Sally's window for a late-night kiss. The trick is to do it without her father finding out. Sally has warned me not to try it.

"Don't do it, Victor," she said. "You know that my father is the best sharpshooter in town."

It's true. Her old man has won the county fair marks-manship tournament for the last five years running. Even those slick city folks who show up every year with their fancy guns and laser scopes can't beat him. I know it's crazy for me to be taking such a risk. But it will all be worth if I get to kiss the lips of my beautiful Sally.

Standing in the way of my late-night amorous ren-dezvous, however, is not only her dad, but a mangy old hound dog named Chip. I'm afraid the dog will hear me as I creep up to Sally's window. If he starts howling and wakes up her dad, I'll be one dead kid. So instead, I sit here up in this tree waiting for the right moment to make my move.

I wait . . . and I wait . . . and I wait. But that darn old Chip never moves from his post. I'm just about ready to give it all up and head home when I see old Chip's ears perk up. The hound dog gives out a low growl and begins to make his way toward the woods in my direction.

Did he see me? I wonder, but old Chip walks right past me, still growling. What great luck! I jump down from the tree and begin my sprint toward Sally's window. I'm about to tap on her window to let her know that I am here when I hear the most horrendous shriek coming from the woods.

Greeehhhh!

That loud shriek is followed by the sound of a loud yelp.

"What's going on out there?" I hear Sally's dad call out from his bedroom window.

I beat a hasty retreat toward the woods and hide behind a bush. Sally's dad steps out from the front door with a shotgun in his hands. I try to sneak away but end up tripping over something and fall down hard on my shoulder. As I look around I realize that I've tripped over poor old Chip, who is lying on his side. Chip is as dead as a doornail! There are two large puncture wounds on the dog's neck. It's as if someone . . . or something . . . has sucked him dry! Instantly I am reminded of the stories Grandma Maya told me back when I was child, about a creature she called the Blood-Sucking Beast. Why any grandmother would think it wise to fill a child's brain with stories of a vicious green-skinned monster that preys upon unsuspecting victims by draining every single drop of blood in their bodies is a mystery to me. But she always said the Blood-Sucking Beast was real. That it stood as tall as a full-grown man and had razor-like claws that were are as sharp as brand-new steak knives, like the ones you see on TV. I hear a hissing sound behind my back. Slowly, I turn to find myself face to face with the very creature from my grandma's stories. Its glowing red eyes stare into mine. I want to run, I really do. But with every step the creature takes, I find it harder and harder to move. It's as if the creature's red eyes have some kind of mind control power over me that's keep me from running. The creature gets closer and closer until it is so close that the drool dripping from monster's mouth falls on my sneakers.

Bang! Bang! The sudden sound of gunfire breaks the monster's hypnotic trance on me. The beast gives out a loud shriek as a bullet finds its mark on his left shoulder. The monster runs away and disappears into the shadows. That's when I see Sally's dad running toward me with his shotgun.

"Are you okay, boy?" he asks me.

"I think so," I whisper, still shaking in fear.

"What in the world was that thing?" he asks me.

"The . . . the . . . the blood . . . the Blood-Sucking Beast," I mumble with great difficulty.

"You're kidding me." He casts a long look in the direction of where the creature once stood. "You mean it's real?

I always figured it to be just a story," he says, scratching his head. "What were you doing out here in the woods, anyway? Don't you have school tomorrow?"

What am I going to tell him? I can't very well say I was here trying to sneak a late-night kiss from his daughter Sally. "I wanted to see if my Grandma Maya's stories about the Blood-Sucking Beast were real."

"Maya?" he asks. "Well, I'll be . . . that would make you Big Mike's boy, wouldn't it?"

"Yes." Everybody calls my dad Big Mike on account of that he's as big as a pro wrestler.

"Your old man and I were best friends back in high school," he tells me. "You shouldn't be out here at night, especially with that thing . . . whatever it was, lurking about. Help me drag poor old Chip back home so we can give him a proper burial. Then we can go inside and call your folks to come pick you up."

Did he just say go inside his house?

"That's a nasty scratch you got on your shoulder," he tells me. "My daughter Sally fancies herself a bit of a nurse. She can bandage you right up, if that's okay with you?"

"Yes, sir," I agree with a smile on my face. Talk about good luck!

"But don't you be making any googly eyes at my daughter. You hear me?"

"I wouldn't dream of it, sir. I wouldn't dream of it."

Tunnels

"Ouch!" I scream as I hit the bottom of the cave. I look up at the night sky through the hole I fell through after being chased by one of the wildest and weirdest looking animals I've ever seen in my life. I reach into my right pocket and pull out a small keychain flashlight. It's not much, but at least I can see what's in front of me now.

"Wait a minute, Joe," I tell myself. "This isn't a cave. It's some sort of tunnel. Man-made, judging from the wooden frame." I look around and find a light switch. I flick it on. "Just how long does this tunnel run?" I ask myself as I stare at the long passageway that is now illuminated in front of me. "Drugs," I think to myself. It has to be. This must be one of those tunnels I've read about in the news. Drug cartels use them to transport drugs into the United States. I need to get out of here and fast. The last thing I want is for drug dealers to catch me wandering around in here. But what about that wild animal that chased me?

I had just wanted to go night fishing in the river behind my grandfather's house. My mom had told me that I shouldn't, that it wasn't safe anymore. She said that drug dealers were using the river to smuggle drugs. What she didn't know was that running into drug dealers wasn't the only danger. Apparently, one also has to worry about the Chupacabras, if that indeed was what I had been chased by earlier.

I've heard stories about the Chupacabras. Supposedly it's a green-skinned alien from outer space that feeds on blood. But if that thing I ran into was the real deal, then the Chupacabras looks more like an oversized, hairless pitbull. Not that it made him any less scary. I remember seeing it one night on a TV show. The footage came courtesy of a police officer's dashboard camera. It showed one of those Chupacabras creatures trying to get away from the patrol car. I remember laughing at it back then. I had even told my dad how fake the creature looked. That it was an obvious hoax. But the Chupacabras I now know is real.

I make my way down the tunnel, hoping that I will reach an exit soon. Am I even going in the right direction? Am I even still in the United States? I could be in Mexico for all I know. As I make my way through the tunnel, I hear the sound of footsteps in front of me. I look quickly for a place to hide, but there really isn't anywhere to do that. Suddenly a boy, not older than nine, jumps out in front of me. He's wearing a tattered T-shirt with the logo of a Mexican soccer team on it. The boy stares at me as if trying to figure out if I present a threat to him or not. I think he's as scared of me as I am of him. Could he have ended up in the tunnels the same way I did? He begins to talk to me in

Spanish. My own Spanish is a bit rusty, but it's good enough for me to communicate with him. I tell him that my name is Joe and that I fell through a hole. And that's how I ended up here. I ask him if the same thing happened to him. He tells me that his name is Martín and that he's down here looking for his dog Chato.

"Did you find him?" I ask in Spanish.

He shakes his head and tells me that he hasn't. I mention to him that we should get out before any drug dealers show up. He tells me that he knows a way out but refuses to leave without his dog Chato. He says he isn't afraid of the drug dealers and that Chato will protect him. I try to explain to him that a dog isn't going to be much protection from a gun, but he won't listen to me. I ask him if he'll show me the way out if I help him find Chato. He agrees.

We call out as we make our way down the tunnel. "Chato! Chato!"

"Maybe he got out already, Martín."

"He wouldn't leave without me."

"Who's there?!" cries out a voice from behind us.

We both turn and see three guys armed with guns coming toward us. The drug dealers!

"Martín, we need to hide," I turn to whisper, but he's already gone.

"You there . . . don't move," shouts one of the men. His gun is pointed in my direction as he makes his way to me.

"What are you doing here, kid?"

"I fell," I tell him. "I was trying to get away from the Chupacabras and I fell in a hole."

"The Chupacabras?"

He turns to look at his two buddies, who are laughing.

"Too bad for you, kid," he says as he raises his gun and points it at my head.

"Grrr . . . grrr . . . grrr . . . !"

"What's that?" asks the guy pointing the gun at my head. He tells the other two guys to go check it.

"Chato," I think to myself. Could it be Martín's dog?

As the two guys make their way down the tunnel, the lights suddenly turn off.

"Who turned off the lights?" the two guys ask. Their question is followed by loud and screeching screaming.

"Aarghh!"

Suddenly the guy standing next to me screams too, and I feel something knock him down to the ground. The lights turn back on. Blood is oozing from his mouth. The same beast that was chasing me earlier is now standing over the drug dealer. It has ripped his throat out and is now licking his blood.

"Chato!" calls out Martín.

I watch as the Chupacabras begins walking toward Martín. It does so slowly at first, but with each step it takes, it seems to run faster and faster. I watch as the Chupacabras leaps at Martín, knocking him down to the ground. The monster then begins to . . . lick Martín's face? The ferocious monster that just moments earlier butchered three men is now playfully licking Martín's face?

"Chato . . . Chato," Martín utters, embracing the creature.

This is Chato? The Chupacabras is Chato?

Martín gestures for me to follow him and Chato down the tunnel. Chato turns and growls at me. But Martín squeezes his neck and makes him stop. As we make our way out of the tunnel, Martín points me in the direction of a Border Patrol watchtower in the distance.

"Go," says Martín, smiling. He then gestures for the Chupacabras to follow him back into the tunnel.

When I make it to the Border Patrol tower, I tell the agents about the tunnel. I tell them about the drug dealers. I even tell them about Martín and the Chupacabras. When they go and check it out, they tell me that they found the tunnel, as well as the bodies of the three dead men. But Martín and the Chupacabras . . . they were nowhere to be seen.

The Devil Is Making Him Do It

"What did you call me?" asks Mr. López.

"I didn't call you anything," Freddie answers, terrified.

He promised his mother this morning that he would not get into trouble at school today. But it sure looks like Freddie is about to break that promise.

Mr. López eyes Freddie suspiciously.

* * *

Poor Freddie; he really is trying to be good. But rest assured that by the time I get done with him, his mother will get that robocall from school to let her know that little Freddie has gotten into trouble again. In the past two days, I've made him skip classes, talk back to his teachers and even set off a firecracker in the middle of the hallway . . . But I've saved the best for last. Today, I will get Freddie to start a food fight in the cafeteria. This will not be just any food fight, mind you, oh no . . . it will be the greatest food fight in the history of all middle schools! It will be monumental! It will be epic! And today being Enchilada Wednesday, it will be especially messy! Why am I doing all these terrible things to Freddie, you ask me? Because getting people into trouble is what I do. It's what I have always done since the dawn of time. Who am I, you ask? You could say that I am the source of inspiration for every foul and vile deed that has ever taken place on the face of this earth. I am . . . the Devil! I'm not speaking metaphorically here. I mean, I am *literally* the Devil. The Fallen Angel, the Prince of Darkness, God's rival. I truly am evil incarnate.

* * *

"Go to the office, Freddie," says Mr. López, very much offended by the bad word he heard directed at him.

The truth is that it was I who uttered that little gem of an obscenity. Did I mention that I am a very gifted ventriloquist? The counselors will blame Freddie's misbehavior on the recent death of his father, Gilberto. Nice guy, Freddie's dad. Former boxer with a killer left cross. He could have gone pro, but he gave up his shot at boxing glory to raise his son, and to his credit he never regretted that decision. He also went to church each and every Sunday without fail. I hate those types of people. I mean, would it kill them to just take a Sunday off every once in a while? Freddy and his dad were close too. It didn't matter how tired he was from work. His old man always made time for his little boy. Any promise that his old man made was golden, and Freddie knew it. His old man always kept his word.

That is, except for the promise that he would always be there for him. That he would never leave him. But when Gilberto died, he left poor Freddie all alone. Freddie understands that his father didn't mean to die. It wasn't his fault that a drunk driver was on the road on the same night as his dad was. But Freddie still feels as if his father has abandoned him somehow. It's an irrational thought, of course. But Freddie is just a kid dealing with the grief of losing his father. As Freddie sits alone in the principal's office waiting for her to arrive, I decide that it's time to make myself known to him.

"They are always picking on you, aren't they, Freddie?"

"Who said that?" asks Freddie. The look on the boy's face is just plain priceless! The boy must think he's losing his mind.

"I said it," I tell him while still invisible.

The boy jumps out of his chair. He's terrified!

"Who said that?"

I slowly begin to materialize in front of him. I'm wearing a red T-shirt. My pants hang almost halfway down my butt. It's silly, I know, and my exposed boxers leave nothing to the imagination. But it's what kids seem to like to wear nowadays, and never let it be said the Devil doesn't keep a sharp eye on the latest teen fashions.

Freddie wants to scream. I can see it on his face.

I raise my index finger to his lips. "Cat got your tongue?" I say to him.

Just like that, Freddie tries to speak, but no words come out.

"Not the cat," I correct myself. "Rather, I've got your tongue." I open my hands and show it to him. I just love freaking people out with that little trick!

"Calm down, Freddie," I tell him. "I bet you're just dying to know who I am and how I did that."

Freddie nods his head.

I jump onto the principal's desk. Maybe it's the artist in me, but I just love being dramatic like that. "I AM THE DEVIL!" I declare.

The boy is truly terrified. I can see it in his eyes. I better tone it down before I make him pee in his pants. It's happened before.

"You don't have to fear me," I tell him. Well, maybe he should . . . just a little.

"I mean you no harm." In my defense, I did cross my fingers behind my back when I said that.

"I am only here to help," I say—or, rather, help myself. "I know you are having difficulties at school, right?" I should know . . . I am causing them!

Freddie nods his head.

"What if I told you I could make it all go away? That I could fix it so nobody could ever hurt you? Would you be interested?"

Freddie doesn't answer. He's as quiet as a mouse.

"Speak up, boy, are you interested or not?"

Silly me, I forgot that I took his tongue. I snap my fingers. "Try talking now."

"You will make sure nothing bad ever happens to me again?" asks Freddie.

"You've got my word."

"How are you going to do that?"

"Let me show you," I tell him just as the school principal walks into the room. "Let's call this a free sample, shall we?"

"What's going on, Freddie?" the principal asks him.

"Nothing . . . "

"According to Mr. López, you called him a pretty nasty word."

"But I didn't do it."

The principal, Mrs. Martínez, walks over to her desk. Freddie notices me standing behind the principal's rolling chair. As she begins to sit down, I pull the chair out from under her.

"Ouch!" she shrieks out in pain as she comes down hard on her tailbone.

"Are you okay?" Freddie is quick to ask her.

"My goodness!" screams the principal's secretary, who has come running into the office. "What happened?"

"Get the nurse!" cries out Mrs. Martínez in pain.

Freddie is sent back to class. "Mrs. Martínez will have to deal with you later," says the secretary.

"See," I tell him. "I kept my promises. You didn't get in trouble."

"But you hurt her," he snaps back at me. "I didn't tell you to hurt her."

"You didn't tell me not to," I remind him.

"I don't want to do this," says Freddie. "This is wrong. Just leave me alone."

"Leave you alone? You really think it's that easy to tell the Devil no?"

"You can't make me do anything I don't want to," says Freddie defiantly.

It's time for me to show this little brat who's really in charge here.

"You're going to do everything I tell you to, Freddie."

I raise my arms up in the air and wave them up and down. Much to Freddie's surprise, his own arms make the same movements as mine.

"You're my puppet," I tell him, "and I'm your puppeteer."

Just then, the bell rings, announcing that it's time for lunch. "It's time to get you fed, Freddie," I tell him. "LET'S GO EAT!"

As I guide Freddie through the lunch line, he's fighting me every step of the way but is losing badly.

"Get the cheesy enchiladas," I tell him. "Ask for extra cheese . . . tons of it." I watch as the cafeteria lady pours a big spoonful of the gooey yellow stuff.

"It's time, Freddie," I whisper to him as he sits down at one of the cafeteria tables. "You are going to grab that plate full of enchiladas with extra cheese and fling it across the room," I demand.

"But what if I hit somebody with it?"

"That's kind of the idea, you silly boy."

"I don't want to do this."

"I am the Devil, and you will do what I tell you to do."

What a stubborn little wimp Freddie is turning out to be. I force him to pick up that plate of cheesy enchiladas. I watch as he rises to his feet and clutches his lunch tray in his hands. He's still hesitant, but he slowly begins to raise it up into the air.

"That's it," I tell him. "Just take careful aim now."

But Freddie just stands there looking like a total fool. "I won't do it," he tells me.

"You don't have a choice," I remind him.

"Help me!" he cries out at the top of his lungs.

"Help?" I question. "Who in the world do you think is going to come help you?"

That's when I notice that everybody in the cafeteria is frozen in place. What's going on? That's when I see him . . . Mr. Goody-Two-Shoes. The spirit of Freddie's dad is standing in the middle of the lunchroom. He is bathed in a golden light and sporting a halo on his head.

"Dad?" asks Freddie in disbelief. "Is that really you?"

"Freddie," I whisper to him in a low growl, "throw that plate of enchiladas!"

I watch as Freddie places his food tray down on the table and pushes it away.

"No!" he screams at me defiantly. "My daddy taught me better than to start a food fight in the cafeteria."

I lunge at Freddie, but before I can grab him, I feel my feet get whacked out from under me by a solid right cross that knocks me for a loop and sends me reeling to the floor. I look up and see Freddie's old man standing in front of me. He is now sporting a pair of exaggeratedly large angel wings. That's when it hits me. Freddie's dad isn't a mere spirit. Gilberto was such a goody-two-shoes in life that when he died and went up to heaven, they made him a guardian angel. Freddie's dad is a guardian angel!

"Is that really you, Dad?" asks Freddie.

"It's me, son."

"But I thought you had abandoned me."

"I will never leave you, son. I am with you . . . even when you can't see me."

"A father's love for his son," I mutter to myself. It makes me sick to my stomach.

"You win this time," I tell both Freddie and his dad as I begin to fade away. I may be the Devil, but even I know better than to pick a fight with a guardian angel. The good guys may have won today . . . but tomorrow?

The Money Tree

"I don't know, Nicolás," says my little brother Robert. "Do you really think it will work?"

"I'm positive it will work," I tell him.

"I'm still not sure," says little Robert again. He's hesitant to accept my words as being the gospel truth.

"Look . . . who's eleven?"

"You are," he answers.

"And you are . . . ?"

"I'm six."

"So who's lived longer?"

"You have."

"So who's going to know more about stuff, huh?"

"You are." Faced with such logic, little Robert begrudgingly gives in. "So what am I supposed to do again?"

"First, you have to dig a hole in the ground that is big enough for you to bury those four coins of yours."

I hand him a shovel. Little Robert starts digging and in just a few minutes the hole is ready. I gesture for him to place the four coins in the hole, but he's still hesitant.

"But these are my coins. My godmother Matilda gave them to me for my birthday."

"You mean your CREEPY godmother Matilda gave them to you for your birthday?"

"She is not creepy," says little Robert.

Matilda is creepy. A real weirdo, if you ask me. She's an aunt who lives in the house next to us. Five years ago, she met and married a man named Tello. Everything had seemed fine at first. They were even little Robert's godparents at his baptism. But after they moved away to Mexico, people said that Tello began to change. That he drank too much and that he didn't want to work anymore. He even became abusive toward Aunt Matilda. He treated her like a prisoner. She finally gathered the courage to leave him. She fled to a town called Catemaco . . . the witch capital of Mexico. There she became involved in magic, tarot cards, Ouija boards, fortune-telling and the like. Rumors began to surface that Matilda had become a witch. Tello went looking for her in Catemaco and was never seen again. It was as if he had disappeared off the face of the earth. Our mom says that those stories aren't true. That they are nasty rumors spread by ignorant people.

"Tía Matilda left Tello because she discovered that he was lazy and a swindler," Mom said. "He was always looking for ways to cheat people out of their money."

Today Aunt Matilda lives in our late grandfather's house with a pet miniature pig that she named . . . Tello. After her husband, I assume.

"Just put the coins in the hole and get this show on the road," I tell little Robert.

"But how do I know this isn't one of your tricks?"

"I am going to explain this just one more time," I say, rolling my eyes. "If we plant these coins in the ground a money tree will grow."

"Are you sure?"

"Of course, I'm sure."

"How sure are you?"

"Look . . . do orange seeds grow into orange trees?"

"Yes."

"And what do they give us?"

"Oranges," little Robert answers.

"Do apple seeds grow into apple trees?"

"Yes."

"And what do they give us?"

"Apples."

"So if we plant these coins in the ground, what kind of trees do you think will grow?"

"Money trees?" asks little Robert.

"And what's going to grow from a money tree?"

"Money," declares little Robert.

The minute I see that greedy little grin come to his face, I know I have him. "Precisely," I tell him. "We'll grow a money tree so large that it will give us thousands of coins. We'll be rich!"

"Okay, let's do it," little Robert decides and places the coins in the hole. He then shovels the dirt back into the hole to cover them up.

"Now, remember, little Robert, you have to water them every day . . . or they won't grow."

"Yes, sir," he says.

Little Robert taps his feet together and salutes like a soldier would.

* * *

Once everyone is asleep, I sneak out of our room and quietly leave the house through the kitchen door. I make my way to the back of our house, where little Robert buried his coins. I start digging for them with my hands until I find them.

"What are you doing out here at night?" a voice asks from behind me, catching me by surprise. I turn and see Aunt Matilda standing there holding Tello.

"Nothing," I quickly tell her, trying to hide the coins behind my back.

"You shouldn't be out here so late at night, Nicolás. It's not safe, you know."

"Not safe?"

"*Brujas* come out at night," she warns me.

"*Brujas*?" I ask her. "What's a *bruja*?"

"In English I believe the word would be . . . witches."

"I didn't know that."

"Did you know that not all witches are evil?" she asks me. "Some actually use their powers to help people or to

teach them a lesson, if they are conniving little thieves, like my husband Tello."

At the mention of the name Tello, her pet pig gives out a loud squeal. *"Squeal! Squeal!"*

"So tell me, Nicolás, do you need to learn a lesson?"

"No," I tell her. "I'm good."

"Really? Then what are you hiding behind your back?"

"Nothing . . . " I answer. Darn . . . she's on to me! She knows I took little Robert's coins. What am I going to do?

Just then, the hooting of an owl that is perched in a tree catches her attention. Taking advantage of her momentary distraction, I place the coins in my mouth.

"Show me your hands," she tells me.

I comply readily and open my hands. She eyes me suspiciously, when suddenly the owl from the tree flies right at me!

"Aaargh!" I scream as I trip and fall hard on my back.

The coins . . . the coins are stuck in my throat. I'm choking! I try to cough them out, but end up swallowing them instead. "Gulp!"

"Are you okay?" asks Matilda.

"The owl . . . why did it attack me?"

Right on cue, my stomach begins to make strange gurgling sounds and starts to hurt. I place my hands on my stomach and feel something moving inside of it. I want to scream, but no words are coming out. Something is moving inside my stomach. I can feel it! Something begins to make its way up my throat. What's happening to me? I open my mouth and see that something is growing out from inside me. What is that? It looks like . . . it looks like . . . twigs? Are those twigs I see growing out of my mouth? The twigs are growing bigger now and starting to sprout leaves! I want to scream for help, but I can't. I'm going to die! Buds appear on the branches growing out of my mouth and instantly open up to reveal . . . coins? There is an actual money tree growing out from inside of me!

"Did you learn your lesson?" asks Aunt Matilda.

I nod my head yes.

Aunt Matilda reaches out and plucks one of the coins from the tree branches. The pain is excruciating and makes me black out.

When I wake up I am lying on the ground on my stomach. I look around, but Aunt Matilda and her pet pig are gone. Feeling as if something is still stuck in my throat, I try to cough it out. I cough into my hands until I feel something finally dislodge itself from my throat. I open up my hands to reveal . . . four coins.

The Devil in Mrs. Leal's Class

"What in the world are you two doing here?" asks Josefina. "I didn't know they let nerds into dance class."

"Anybody can take dance class, Josefina," I tell her.

"That's right," says my best friend, Angelina. "Marta and I have as much right to be here as anybody else."

The truth is neither one of us wants to be here. But the school counselor told us that we needed to take a physical education class as part of our curriculum, so it was either this or volleyball class. Neither one of us is very athletically gifted, so between getting hit on the head with a volleyball and tripping over our own two feet in dance class . . . we decided to go with what we viewed as being the lesser of two evils.

"Just don't let anybody know you are my cousin," she tells me. "It's embarrassing enough already to have a nerd for a cousin." Josefina rolls her eyes as she walks away.

"She is so stuck-up," says Angelina.

"I know," I tell her.

It's true. Josefina is the most stuck-up girl in school. Unfortunately, she is also my cousin. Josefina is one of the most beautiful girls in the entire school. Every guy is drooling over her, and she knows it, too. Josefina likes to make all the guys compete for her affection. She also likes it when they fight over her. She especially loves that. She likes to brag that she can have any guy she wants. What's worse is that if she finds out that a guy likes me, she'll go and start flirting with him just to make sure he won't talk to me. My mom said that she acts that way because she is jealous of me.

"But why would Josefina be jealous of me?" I asked my mom. "She is the one who is beautiful."

"You are beautiful too, *m'ija*," my mom told me. "But you are also smart. Beauty will fade with time, Marta, but being smart will last forever."

"Everybody line up," says Mrs. Leal as she enters the room. "Today we will be learning ballroom dancing."

"Do you want me to warm up the class, Mrs. Leal?" asks Josefina.

"Teacher's pet," whispers Angelina to me.

"Sure, Josefina," says Mrs. Leal.

Knock . . . knock.

"Somebody's knocking at the door," I tell Mrs. Leal.

"Come in," she says.

A tall young boy wearing a cowboy hat and blue jeans walks into the dance studio. He politely takes off his hat before addressing Mrs. Leal.

"Is this Mrs. Leal's dance class?" asks the young man.

"He's gorgeous," Angelina whispers in my ear. "Just look at that smile and those blue eyes."

She's right. He's by far the most handsome boy I've ever seen in the entire school.

"Yes," says Mrs. Leal, "you're in the right place."

"Nice to meet you, Mrs. Leal," he tells her and shows her his class schedule. "My name is Thomas, but everyone just calls me Tommy." The young man gently reaches out and shakes Mrs. Leal's hand.

"Well, look at you," says Mrs. Leal. "You guys could stand to learn a thing or two about manners from Tommy here."

Mrs. Leal's words make Tommy blush ever so slightly. Needless to say, that causes every girl in the room to let out a collective "How cute," and we feel our hearts melt.

"So have you ever taken a dance class before?" Mrs. Leal asks.

"Not really," he answers. "But you could say that I know my way around a ballroom. I get it from my old man. My dad is a very good dancer. In his younger days he had a reputation for setting many a dance floor on fire."

"Really?" asks Mrs. Leal. "Well maybe you can show us a little bit of what you know?"

"It would be my honor," he tells her. "Maybe somebody in class could be my partner so I can demonstrate what I know? How about you?" he asks, pointing at me.

"Me?" I say. "But I can't dance. It's my first day in class."

"Anybody can dance," he insists. Staring at him, I can't help but lose myself in those blue eyes of his.

"But where are my manners?" he tells me. "I don't even know your name."

"Marta . . . my name is Marta."

"Well, Marta, may I have the honor of this dance?"

Before I even realize what I am doing, I am in front of to him.

"Just follow my lead," he whispers in my ear. He winks at me and flashes that mischievous little boy grin of his.

"I would follow you anywhere," I think to myself. Seconds later I am dancing. I mean I am actually dancing!

"Left . . . right . . . left . . . right and turn," he instructs.

I am actually doing it! I am dancing . . . and I'm good at it, too! I look around the room. All eyes are upon us. My best friend, Angelina, is smiling at me. My cousin Josefina is staring at me too . . . and boy, does she look super jealous! But I don't care! I'm dancing! Really dancing! I'm dancing with the most handsome guy in the entire school . . . and that's when my world comes crashing down on me.

"Ouch!" I cry out as I trip and land embarrassingly on my butt.

Everybody starts to laugh at me. Did somebody just trip me? I look across from me and see my cousin Josefina looking all innocent-like.

"You tripped me!" I tell her.

"Don't blame me for you being a klutz," she fires back. "You tripped over your own elephant feet."

"That was very good, Tommy," says Mrs. Leal, seemingly not the least bit concerned over my embarrassing fall.

"Tommy, you're a natural!"

"Thank you, Mrs. Leal," says Tommy before going down on one knee to make sure I am all right. "Are you okay, pretty lady?" he asks me.

"I'm okay," I say. I am so embarrassed I can't even look at him.

"I'd like to see how you do with a dance partner who has more dancing experience," says Mrs. Leal. "Josefina . . . are you ready?"

Before Mrs. Leal can even finish her question, Josefina is dragging Tommy to the middle of the classroom. Together they move in perfect rhythm, twisting and turning to the beat of the music that plays from Mrs. Leal's CD player.

"Perfect!" cries out Mrs. Leal. "You two look perfect together."

Those words make my heart break. Josefina is going to win—again.

Tommy begins to spin Josefina around the dance floor. He spins her faster and faster. Josefina is laughing at first, but begins to get dizzy and begs him to stop. But Tommy won't stop. He only laughs at her.

"Stop, Tommy!" screams Mrs. Leal.

But Tommy won't listen to her either. He spins faster and faster until, as amazing as it sounds, he and Josefina are just blurs.

"*El Diablo*, he's the Devil!" we hear Josefina scream at the top of her lungs.

Josefina and Tommy both erupt into a giant fireball that reaches all the way to the ceiling, setting off the sprinkler system! But just as suddenly as the fireball erupts in the room, it disappears, leaving no trace of either Josefina or Tommy. The only thing left as proof of what has just happened is a burn mark on the middle of the dance floor. Later, I find a note addressed to me in my backpack. It reads, "Thanks for the dance, pretty lady. Till next time. Lovingly yours, Tommy."

The Selfie

"We shouldn't be here," I tell Rudy as I follow him through a broken window into the room. Abandoned for years, the old tax office at Fort Ringgold is covered in dust and cobwebs.

"Stop being such a chicken, Mateo," says Rudy, pointing a flashlight at my face. "We both agreed to do it."

"No, YOU agreed to do it," I remind him. "I'm just the idiot that you talked into tagging along with you."

"This way," he tells me, gesturing for me to follow him down a flight of stairs. "The room would have been down in the basement."

"Should we really be doing this?" I ask him. "I mean, do we really want to be messing with ghosts?"

"I thought you said that you don't believe in ghosts."

"I don't."

"Then you've got nothing to be afraid of, right?"

I certainly hope so, but I've got this nagging feeling that maybe I am afraid of something.

"So what's the story with this place? What is so scary about an old tax office?"

"It wasn't always a tax office," says Rudy. "It used to be a hospital during the Civil War."

"A hospital? I never knew that."

"My grandma says that back when she used to work here as a secretary, she and her coworkers heard strange noises."

"Like what?"

"They heard voices . . . footsteps . . . the usual stuff," he tells me as he scans the basement with his flashlight. All we see are old desks and tables. "What she says was really scary was when they heard the screaming."

"Screaming . . . what do you mean, screaming?"

"'Cries of agony' are what my grandma called them. Many soldiers died while medics were trying to save them. Their deaths were so traumatic that their souls became trapped in this world."

"That's creepy," I tell him.

"Hey, that's what my grandma told me," says Rudy.

"Let's just get this over with."

"This looks like a good spot." He points the flashlight at a desk in the middle of the room.

"Fine by me," I tell him, taking out my cell phone.

We both climb onto the desk and pose together for a selfie that will prove to our friends that we indeed took the dare and went into the basement of the old tax office.

"Hold it up high," says Rudy. "I want you to get as much of the room as possible."

"Say, 'cheese,'" I tell him as I snap the picture.

The phone's flash momentarily floods the room with light.

"Got it," I tell Rudy. "Now let's get out of here . . . this place gives me the creeps."

We hurriedly make our way up the stairs but find that the door we came through is now locked.

"Did you lock the door, Rudy?"

"No. I don't even remember closing it. It must have been you."

"I didn't lock it," I tell him. "It had to have been you!"

"It wasn't me," says Rudy.

"If it wasn't you . . . then who did it?"

"How am I supposed to know?!" he screams back at me. "All I know is that it wasn't me!"

"Help me . . . " a voice whispers, from down the stairs.

"What was that?" asks Rudy.

"I don't know. It came from down the stairs. Point the flashlight down there."

"Help me . . . " says another voice, a different one this time.

"There's nobody down there!" says Rudy.

"Help me . . . help me . . . help me . . . " We're hearing even more voices now coming from every corner of the basement.

"There's nobody down there!" screams Rudy as he continues to point his flashlight in the direction of the basement. "There's nobody down there!"

I turn and begin to fiddle with the door knob, trying to force it open.

"Help us, help us," the voices begin to chant.

"They're getting closer," says Rudy. "They're coming up the stairs!"

Just then, the doorknob turns in my hands, and I swing the door open.

"Let's go!" I scream at Rudy.

We both run toward the broken window we had used to sneak into the building.

"What was that down there?" I ask Rudy.

"I don't know, Mateo, but let's get out of here," says Rudy as we finish climbing out the window.

We run and run until we're far enough not to see the old tax office anymore.

"What just happened?" asks Rudy. "Those voices that we heard . . . were they ghosts?"

"I don't know what they were," I tell him. "I just know that I don't want to ever go back in there again."

"Your phone," asks Rudy. "We did take a picture, right?"

"Sure."

I pull the phone out of my pocket. I begin flipping through my photographs until I come across a picture that nearly makes my heart skip a beat.

"What's wrong?" asks Rudy. "Don't tell me it didn't come out."

I want to speak, but I'm in too much of a shock to put into words what I am seeing.

"What's wrong?" asks Rudy. "Tell me, Mateo . . . please!"

I hand my phone over to him and show him what I am looking at. The picture shows both of us smiling like idiots for the camera, but that isn't what's got me so scared. All around us in the photograph are soldiers . . . dead soldiers.

Can I Keep Him?

"I found a dog," I tell my mother. "Can I keep him? I'll take care of him. I promise."

"You know we can't keep a dog, Nikko," she tells me. "Your dad doesn't like dogs."

"But that's not fair," I tell her. "Martín isn't even my dad. I hate him."

"You shouldn't say things like that."

"Why not?" I ask her. "Because he'll hit me like he does you?"

"Don't say that, Nikko."

"Why not? It's true."

My stepdad, Martín, is as mean as they come. He's nothing but a drunk. Every time he comes home, he reeks of beer, and all he ever does is call my mom all sorts of nasty names. Sometimes I wish I was big enough to be able to punch him in the nose.

"It's not fair, Mom," I tell her. "All my friends have dogs."

"I know they do," she says.

"But he is so cute. . . . Let me show him to you."

I lean down and pick him up in my arms. My mom stares at me funny, like she's confused or something.

"I see," she says hesitantly.

"I'm going to call him Vinnie," I say. "Do you want to pat him on the head? He likes that."

"Sure," she says, smiling as she leans over and pats Vinnie on his head. "I guess there's no chance of your stepdad ever finding out about Vinnie, right? So let's go ahead and keep him."

"Hooray!" I cry out. "Let's go to my room, Vinnie. I'm going to show you where you're going to sleep from now on!"

I spend the entire day playing with Vinnie. We run around in the backyard chasing after squirrels. I try to teach him to fetch, but Vinnie can't get the hang of it. I end up having to go and pick up the stick myself each time I throw it. But I'm sure he'll figure it out eventually. When I take Vinnie for a walk, some of the bigger kids in the neighborhood make fun of us and call me a weirdo for no reason. Vinnie growls at them, but I tell him to leave them alone. Bigger kids like to make fun of smaller kids just to be mean.

Vinnie is such a good dog that he doesn't even need a leash when I walk him. He just follows alongside me. He's the best dog in the whole wide world. I knew he would be from the first moment I saw him playing around in the pet cemetery. He ran right up to me and practically jumped right into my arms. I knew at that exact moment that he would be my dog forever . . . till death do us part.

By the time Vinnie and I get back home, I can hear my stepdad's voice coming from inside the house. He's yelling at my mom. The sound of my dad screaming makes Vinnie so mad that he begins to growl. When we walk into the house my stepdad is about to hit Mom, but I yell for him to stop.

"Leave my mom alone!"

"Did you just yell at me?!" he shouts at me as he begins to remove his leather belt from his pants. "That's the problem with you kids today. You don't respect your elders. But I'll teach you to respect me, boy."

"Stay away from me," I warn him. "Stay away or I'll tell my dog Vinnie to bite you!"

"Dog? What dog? I didn't say you could have a dog!"

"But I do have a dog now," I tell him. "And he's right here! "

"Where? I don't see anything."

"Right here," I tell him, pointing at my leg. "He's right here, and he'll bite you if you don't leave us alone right now."

"You're crazy," he half laughs as he grabs me by my shirt and pulls me toward him. "I'll teach you to make up stuff!"

Just then Vinnie begins to growl and jumps at my stepdad, sinking his teeth deep into his arm!

"Aaaay!" he screams.

Vinnie bites him on both his ankles and then goes for his legs and thighs. My stepdad is screaming in pain as he begins to crawl toward the door, trying to get away from Vinnie, who is on him like a wolf.

"Get it off me, get it off me!" He screams as he opens the living room door and takes off, but not before Vinnie gives him one last bite right on the butt!

"Good dog," I tell Vinnie, "good dog."

"What's going on?" asks my mother. "How did you do that?"

"How did I do what?" I ask her.

"What you did to your dad? How did you do that?"

"But I didn't do anything, Mom. It was Vinnie."

"But Vinnie isn't real," she says.

"What do you mean Vinnie isn't real? He is right here next to me."

"But there's no dog next to you, Nikko. When you showed me your dog earlier . . . there was no dog in your arms. I thought he was an imaginary friend."

"But Vinnie is real," I tell her. "He's sitting right next to you, Mom. He's licking your hand . . ."